Prelude to a Storm

Cecily Magnon

To the best brother in the world. Love you! Tg "Cecily"

DEDICATION

To my husband and kids, I do this for you. I love you guys!

To Nancy and Alita, what can I say; but this dream wouldn't be where it is without you. I love you both!

CONTENTS

1 CHAPTER ONE
MID JULY, 1984

Sarah sighed deeply, looking at the long stretch of road ahead of her. Her right hand loosely held the steering wheel and her left arm leaned against the window as she and her best friend sped down the freeway to start their "summer-to-remember."

She was contemplating what she wanted to do with her life. She was only seventeen, just graduated, and right now, right this moment, all she knew was that she was up for an adventure. She felt excited over the current feeling of freedom and she wanted to relish in the moment. Her parents were incredibly strict and she didn't know when this type of "gift" would come upon her again.

"Oh. My. God! We're gonna totally have so much fun!" Samantha smacked her gum loudly.

She looked at her friend. The girl was moving her head in circles to catch different parts of her face in the small sun-visor mirror. She applied her bright red lipstick and puckered her lips into a tissue. Sarah smiled at her friend's preening habits and wondered how Samantha ever got herself out of the house on time. Her hair alone took at least one can of hairspray before Sam was satisfied that the stiff waterfalls she called bangs would actually hold their shape.

Sarah reached for the cassette sticking out of the player and pushed it in. She heard it click and the wheels started winding to play a song.

Like a virgin. Touched for the very first time…

Samantha squealed in delight, turning the volume up on the car stereo. "I love this song! I love Madonna! She's totally fearless." She looked into the mirror again and fluffed her hair, "If I dyed my hair blonde, I could totally look like her."

Sarah looked over at Samantha posing in front of the miniature mirror. "You're way prettier," she snorted, stifling a chuckle, "but you sound like a cat in heat when you sing."

Samantha shrugged, ignoring her last comment. She was back to fixing her make-up. After a moment, she turned slowly, looked at Sarah, the twinkle in her eyes shining with mischief. She raised an eyebrow and a smirk curled the corner of her glossy red lips. "Van didn't seem to mind…"

Sarah's eyes darted between her friend and the road. Her expression turned suspicious. "Ok, spill."

Samantha blushed, her face matching the redness of her lips. She giggled nervously.

She could hear Samantha gulp. "What is it?"

"Whew!" Samantha blew out, fanning herself with her hand. "I'm hot! Is the A/C on?"

She eyed her friend suspiciously. "Samantha Montclair," her tone was accusatory. She raised an eyebrow herself, realization dawning on her. "You didn't!?"

Samantha buried her face in her hands, "Yes! I did!" she groaned, her voice muffled.

Sarah laughed and hooted.

Samantha groaned and slumped down in her seat. She looked miserable.

Sarah waggled her eyebrows. "So, how was it? You have to tell me!" She poked her friend's side.

"I'm still sore!" Samantha was trying to stifle a laugh. "Oh my god, it hurt!"

Sarah couldn't stop smiling at her friend.

"… but I would totally do it again!"

This was going to be a fun day. They'd left early in the morning, telling Samantha's parents they wanted to get an early start shopping and would be gone all day. Of course, they didn't say, they would be shopping in Tijuana, but… Sam's parents didn't ask.

They were almost to their destination. The Mexican border was only about a mile away and they had to start looking for a parking lot. Sarah was still trying to interrogate Sam when she spotted a lot not too far from the border. She began to slow down and turned into the gated space.

She was still prodding for info as they readied to cross the border.

She'd never been with a boy and was dying to know what sex was like; that her best friend was withholding information from her was a form of unnecessary torment.

"Saaaam. Tell me."

"There's nothing to tell." Samantha's face scrunched up. "It wasn't all that good."

"You said you'd do it again!"

"Well, yeah, but I didn't say it was good."

"What?" she asked.

"We were done in like a minute! Seriously. I don't even think he kissed me," Samantha huffed.

"Oh." Sarah was disappointed at the news. She thought it would be more meaningful, more special, and more breathtaking than that. "Well that sucks."

"That's what Van should have been doing to me!" Sam chuckled. "Instead of just poking me. I swear, I thought he was having a seizure!" Sam rubbed the back of her head. "I had the worst headboard headache. I think I've got a goose egg back there." She groaned. "Ech! Never again with that guy."

Sarah was laughing now, "Oh my god." She wiped at her eyes, "Come on Madonna, let's go."

They decided to travel light, anticipating that they would be doing a lot of walking. They each brought a backpack and made sure they only brought the essentials -- cameras, IDs, and money. They twined their arms together and began their entry into Mexico on foot, both girls giddy with excitement. From the parking lot to the border was only a block, and once across they hailed a taxi to take them to Tijuana's famous market place.

"Avenida Revolución, por favor." Sarah said to the cab driver. Her

Spanish sounded a lot better than she thought it would; four years of Spanish class with Sam was finally paying off.
"Impressive, Ms. Amalfi," her friend snickered.

The cab driver simply nodded from his seat and waited for the girls to get into the back of the cab.

He watched them settle in from his rear view mirror, his dark eyes looking impatiently at the girls. "Cierra la puerta," he demanded.

Sam scowled, not appreciating being bossed around. She slammed the door, rocking the old thinned door panels underneath the window. The car frame shook, knocking the little green fragrant tree, off a jimmy-rigged hook, taped against the door.

The cab lurched forward, tires screeching. The driver leered menacingly at them as he merged into tightly packed traffic.

Sarah's eyes widened, her nails digging into the seat. She caught the driver's stare within the rear view mirror and gasped out, "Perdón, señor," hoping her apology would calm the driver.

The dark eyes squinted at her through the rear view mirror, and gave no heed to slowing down. He looked away from her and swerved sharply to the left. Sam fell to the floor, and Sarah slid hard to the right, hitting the other door panel with a thud. Sarah grabbed for Sam's arm to help her back into the seat. "Apologize," Sarah gritted out.

Sam huffed at her and rolled her eyes before catching the driver's attention, "Disculpame, Señor," Samantha droned out.

The cab started to slow, the driver's temper seeming to cool with Sam's apology, the ride becoming less jerky from frequent and abrupt stops. Sarah released her nails from the vinyl seat and finally let out her tightly held breath.

"Gracias, Señor." Sarah offered. She was dizzy and her stomach felt queasy from the rough ride. She leaned her head back against the seat, closed her eyes, and hoped that the ride would soon be over. Of all the drivers in Tijuana, they had to get one with a quick temper.

She felt Samantha's arm next to hers. She leaned away wanting more room while she caught her breath, but then changed her mind and decided to hit Sam on the shoulder. "You almost got us killed."

"I didn't do anything." Sam said innocently, then started talking non-stop about all the shops she wanted to visit, and to remind her to get souvenirs for everyone, and to make sure that she didn't drink any water, and to make sure she got a picture with a Tijuana Zonkey.

Was this really happening? How could Sam be this cheerful after that ride? Sarah peered at her with one eye open. "Zonkey?" she asked, completely perplexed. "What is a zonkey?"

"They are way cool! You can only find them in T.J. It's a local tradition," Sam replied back with a smile.

"What are they?"

Sam chuckled and replied matter of factly, "Zonkeys are donkeys painted to look like zebras."

"What?!"

"Hahaha! Yeah, they're great. They're supposed to be everywhere; pulling around these colorful carts and stuff. Hopefully, it won't take us long to find one," she replied as she looked out her window.

The taxi started to slow and pulled over next to a crowded sidewalk. "Avenida Revolución," the driver spit out.

Sam slid out of the car quickly and onto the sidewalk while Sarah paid for their fare. "Gracias, Señor," she said politely before exiting the backseat.

The driver turned quickly and grabbed Sarah's arm, his dark eyes penetrating her. "Ten cuidado, Señorita. Hay cosas malas que andan por estas calles." *Be careful. There are bad things walking these streets.* His stare softened as he released her arm.

Sarah stared back at the man. Her brows furrowed in confusion. She hesitated leaving the cab, wanting to ask the driver some questions.

"Sarah, hurry up already!" Sam whined impatiently.

The driver nodded at Sarah and smiled tightly. "Ten cuidado." *Be careful.* He turned around to face away from Sarah.

She slipped out and stood next to Sam, watching the taxi pull out into traffic.

"That was weird," she said under her breath.

"Hmm, what?" Sam asked.

She shook her head, her eyes still trailing the taxi. "Nothing. Let's go."

The morning at the Avenida went by quickly and both Sarah and Sam were famished from hours of shopping. Shopping had been uneventful, much to her relief. She'd felt paranoid the entire time, watching over their shoulders and looking for anything suspicious.

She felt tired and wanted a break. The afternoon sun was beating down; the glaring rays making it feel hotter than it was. Sarah shielded her eyes with her hand as she looked around. The crowd was thinning out, everyone seeming to migrate towards areas of shade. That meant the restaurants with air-conditioning would be packed with people.

She looked to her friend. Sam had been quiet for a while; a sure sign that she was tired and hungry. They both needed a break. "Let's go over there." Sarah pointed toward a block with a row of faded pastel buildings.

Sam shrugged her agreement and followed behind her.

They crossed the steaming streets out of the Avenida and toward a two story faded blue building. The building wavered from Sarah's sight. She rubbed her eyes. "This heat is getting bad. Come on, let's hurry and get inside." She pulled at her friend's arm. "Come on, you can make it," she coaxed.

"Uugh! It is sooo hot!"

They ran to the front of the building. An aged wooden sign hung haphazardly above the door. It looked ready to fall, but somehow held on with the remaining strength of the rusted nails poking out of the corners. They crossed the threshold, Sarah looking up, hoping that the "Restaurante" sign wouldn't fall on their heads.

She breathed a sigh of relief as cool air hit her body. They walked tentatively inside the small restaurant and sat down at the only available table.

It felt like paradise inside the restaurant and she immediately relaxed. She looked around and appreciated the age of the space. It was old and felt full of history. At the far end of the restaurant was a beautiful wooden counter that looked hand hewn with intricate carvings on the bar's curved lip and on its wide front panels. Atop the counter was an old fashioned cash register, the kind with an ornate brass metal casing and big round ebony buttons.

Sarah could easily imagine old time vaqueros coming in to the building and leaning on that counter to wait for a drink after a hard day of herding cattle. She looked closer at the carvings gracing the bar and wondered what era it was from. It looked really old.

She started rummaging inside her backpack looking for a pamphlet she'd picked up at the Cultural Center. They'd wanted to take a break from shopping this morning, and the museum seemed like a good place to go. "Sam, do you have that flyer from the museum?"

"No, I didn't keep it. Why?"

"That counter." She jutted her chin toward the bar. "It's beautiful. I just thought the carvings looked similar to the Olmec exhibit we looked at. Remember the one with the big heads?"

Sam shrugged, uninterested. "I'm starving," she groaned.

She set down her backpack and started looking at the pinkish walls of the restaurant. She was starving, too. Her stomach felt like it was eating itself from lack of food. They should have eaten before they left, but they'd been too excited and wanted to get out before Sam's parents started asking questions.

Sam had been tapping her fingers on the table impatiently when a voluptuous woman with honey colored skin and bright red lips came out from a darkened room behind the counter. The woman had her black hair pulled into a tight bun with a bright red, silk flower tucked behind her ear. The woman cooled herself with an accordion fan as she approached them. She looked annoyed that she had been disturbed from whatever she might have been doing.

The woman waddled to their table and closed her fan with a snap of her wrist. She stood next to the small table, her heavy presence looming over them. She eyed them both, pulled out a note pad and pencil from her apron pocket and waited for the girls to place their order.

"¿Qué se les ofrece?" the woman asked, irritated.

The girls looked at the woman in confusion.

"Menu?" Sam asked.

The woman rolled her eyes before letting out a frustrated sigh. Her red lips puckered to the side. "Weelyam!" the woman bellowed in the air.

They looked at each other, two pairs of eyes growing wide in unison as they tried to stifle nervous giggles.

The woman scowled at them. "Weelyam!" she yelled out again. Her shrill voice making the hairs on Sarah's arm stand up in attention.

The girls immediately quieted down when a handsome young man with chin length dark hair and piercing silvery-blue eyes came running to their table. He didn't look that much older than them, but he carried an air of maturity about him. He pushed one side of his hair behind his ears before flashing a smile that should have been illegal.

Sarah was captivated.

"Buenas tardes, Señoritas. How may I help you?"

He spoke perfect English -- no accent. Sarah wondered how he came to be there. It was clear that he worked at the restaurant. He had a dish rag thrown over his shoulder and a small apron tied around his waist. Was the woman his mother? Maybe he looked more like his father?

"Um, we don't know what to order. We didn't get menus," Sam whispered loudly. She looked guardedly at the woman scowling at them from behind the counter.

'Weelyam' chuckled and placed a hand over his tight abdomen. "Be careful, she's got ears like a bat. She hears everything!" he whispered back to Sam.

Sam gulped and looked nervously at Sarah who'd been gazing at the dark haired boy before her.

Sarah couldn't keep her eyes off of him. There was something about his presence that drew her attention and made her notice every detail of his face, his smile, his hair, his voice, his eyes…

He looked at her.

She held her breath as he locked onto her eyes and held them. She felt her face warm with a blush, as images of him invaded her mind.

Eres hermosa, mi angel. My beautiful angel. Her whole body warmed and her heart pounded wildly. Did he say that out loud? No, Sam had been talking to him this entire time; but it felt so real. She thought she felt his breath next to her ear.

"Sarah!" Sam called out. "Yoohoo, Earth to Sarah!"

"Oh, umm…" Sarah stammered realizing that she had been staring at him this whole time.

He looked to her and smiled, showing off deep dimples that just multiplied his level of hotness. "I would recommend the tacos. They're delicious," he said politely.

"That sounds great! We'll have two orders and two sodas," Sam chimed in.

"Great choice. I'll be right back." Sam beamed at 'Weelyam,' watching him walk to the room behind the counter.

"You are totally into him!" Sam snickered.

"What? Nooo. No, I'm not," she lied.

"He's super fine! Tall, dark, and smoldering. Did you see the guns

15

on those arms?!" Sam said loudly. "Ooh. You should invite him to help us find a zonkey. It's the last thing on my list. And then, I can get lost for a while, and you can get all sweet with him." Sam was chuckling.

"Shhh. He'll hear you." She was trying to quiet her friend, but Sam was in a teasing mood now. Sarah cupped her face, feeling her cheeks burn under her fingers. She was trying to ignore Sam's kissy noises and didn't notice him come back to their table. She almost fell out of her chair to hear his voice.

"Are you ok?" he asked. "I have your sodas..." he was hesitating, "...would you like some water or ice?"

Across the table, Sam was shaking her head no, mouthing, "Don't drink the water."

Sarah could feel him staring at her. She could feel his eyes drilling into her, making her insides flutter. She finally turned to look at him and their gaze met. He looked truly concerned.

Sarah felt absorbed by him, his eyes peeling away layers of her soul to see what was inside. She felt crazy. That wasn't possible, but his eyes made her feel like he understood her, understood her dreams, her aspirations, and her quirks.

"I'm ok. Just hot," she said softly. She looked at Sam, who was mouthing "hot, hot, hot," fanning herself, and sneaking mischievous looks at 'Weelyam.'

"I'm glad you're ok." He nodded slightly. "The food will be ready soon." He looked at her one more time, before turning to leave.

"Sam! What if he saw you?!"

"Whaat?! I was hot, too!" Sam chortled loudly. "When he comes back, I'm going to ask for his name and number!"

"No! Sam!"

"Yes! You're such a chicken. That guy is so into you!" Sam's smile was making Sarah nervous.

'Weelyam' came back with two plates of steaming food. He set the plates down carefully in front of the girls and smiled. "Disfruten, enjoy." The girls gawked at their plates and looked at 'Weelyam.' He seemed pleased at their surprise.

Their mouths were salivating at the bright plate of food he'd brought them. The plate was laden with fresh crisp salad, two small soft tacos, and a small cup of savory rice, jeweled with green and red bell peppers.

He started to turn to leave, but Sam stopped him.

"Wait. Weelyam?" Sam was exaggerating the accent. "Is that really your name?" She took a bite of her taco, the juices from the chicken dripping down her fingers. "I'm Sam and that's my best friend, Sarah," pointing her taco at Sarah.

He smiled, placed a hand over his heart and bowed. "I'm sorry. I didn't properly introduce myself. My name is William Koraki. Please, call me Will."

"Koraki?" Sam's eyebrows crinkled, "That doesn't sound Spanish."

"It's Greek." Will said.

"Ooh. A living Greek god," Sam teased. "What are you doing here amongst the mortals? Is that your mom? You don't look like her."

Will simply smiled and started to leave, but Sam stopped him again. "I'll stop. I swear." She crossed her heart and fluttered her eyelashes at him. "Just one more question?" Sam asked in her sweetest, most sincere voice.

"Si, Señorita," he replied patiently. The Spanish rolling off his tongue like honey.

"Can my friend have your phone number?" Sam asked with a bright smile.

Sarah was not smiling. Her stomach tightened, exciting the already frenzied butterflies in her gut. She wanted to vanish into thin air. She was going to feed Sam to a zonkey.

Will looked at her and then at Sam. "I can do better. If the two of you would allow me to accompany you after lunch, for a short time. I can make sure you're both safe." His eyes flicked to the window at the front of the restaurant. "There's been a lot of strange activity around here lately and it's really not safe for two young women to be by themselves."

"We'd love your company, but it's broad daylight. What could happen?" Sam asked.

Sarah's heart was pounding. She'd felt safe, relaxed since they'd been at the restaurant, and... she gulped, remembering the taxi driver's warning about bad things walking the streets. *Hay cosas malas que andan por estas calles,"* the man had said.

"Enjoy your lunch. Take your time. When you're ready, I'll make sure you get safely back over the border." Will gave them a gracious bow before leaving them with their meal.

"Hmmm. You think he's serious?" Sam asked.

Sarah sagged in her chair, beginning to feel uneasy. The air itself felt like it was changing, getting heavy. She rubbed her arms and looked to Sam in all seriousness. "Yeah, I think he is."

The girls ate lunch slowly, neither one in a hurry to leave the shelter of the restaurant. After about an hour of them sitting and staring at their empty plates, the voluptuous woman came back out and slammed their ticket down with a heavy hand. "Chu pay and go!" She turned and squeezed her ample hips in between the aisle of tables to head to the cash register.

The girls hesitantly got up when Will came out from the back room, slinging a duffle bag over a shoulder. He smiled brightly at the girls and motioned for them to stay where they were. Will turned to the woman at the register and flashed a devilish smile.

She gave him a knowing look. He took her hand and placed a chaste kiss on top of her fat fingers. She pulled her hand back and smacked him playfully on the shoulder, saying "Sácate! Pero ten cuidado!"

She wanted them to be careful.

Will walked toward the girls, but turned around one more time to spy on his friend at the register. She had her arms crossed over her full bosoms and her left eyebrow raised all the way to the middle of her forehead. She watched the trio closely as they exited the restaurant.

"Don't worry Rosa! We'll be fine," Will yelled out.

Once outside, the trio started to walk toward the Avenida. Sam broke the silence during their walk and asked Will, "So what's been going on around here that you have to chaperone us?"

Will didn't answer, but looked towards Sarah who was avoiding making eye contact with him.

Sam was walking slow and falling behind Sarah and Will. "Like, has there been a lot of crime? Drugs, kidnapping, robberies, what?" she asked.

Will stopped walking and waited for Sam to catch up to him.

Sarah hadn't noticed him stopping and kept walking ahead.

"Sarah!" he screamed out. She turned quickly toward Will. A

strong wave of energy rushed at her as he ran in her direction. Her heart raced too fast, making breathing difficult.

Danger was near, she could feel it.

Get down! Will's voice was a command in her mind -- clear and spoken with so much force that she had to obey.

Sarah looked towards the direction of the Avenida. A man was heading for them at a fast clip. He looked like a bull aimed straight for a waving red cape.

"Oh. My. God!" Sarah uttered. Fear spiked her nerves.

The man's eyes glowed white in the distance. *Yes, bow down to me, Beautiful!* The bullish man jeered in her mind.

She suddenly felt Will next to her, blocking her on one side. Her scalp tingled with Will's voice in her mind. He was calm, but full of authority. *Run Sarah. Take Sam back to the restaurant.*

Sarah crawled away from behind Will's legs. She struggled to get up and run, as loose gravel slid from beneath her sandals. She finally found her momentum, after all the dust she'd kicked up and hurried to reach Sam.

She pulled Sam quickly back to the restaurant. It was empty of patrons as Rosa stood by the door, waving for them to hurry up and get in. She slammed the door shut and locked it quickly with a large skeleton key.

Without delay, Rosa walked towards the center of the small dining room and stretched her arms to either side of her full figure, her palms facing the ceiling. She dipped her chin toward her chest and began to chant words, foreign to both Sarah and Samantha's ears. The chanting was rhythmic and melodic, reminding Sarah of something tribal.

The chant started soft, only audible as a whisper, but grew louder, stronger, and more intense. The air inside the restaurant sizzled with electricity, the charge sparking the air like stars in the daylight. Rosa brought her arms in quickly, clapping her hands with power.

Warm air rushed at Sarah and Sam, their hairs blowing back from the gust created by Rosa's clap.

Sam was transfixed, looking at Rosa with wonder and excitement. Sarah put her hand lightly on her friend's shoulder, keeping her in place while Rosa rushed to the store front window and peeked out.

Both girls quickly followed suit and squeezed next to Rosa for what available space was left. "Dios mio!" Rosa exclaimed as she made the sign of the cross.

Across the street, Will and a bull-like man were facing off. The man was as tall as Will, but the aggressor was thick and bursting with muscles. The man looked crazy and completely drowned in rage.

Sarah wondered if he was on drugs. She'd heard a lot of news reports lately about people becoming uncontrollable and violent when they took PCP, Angel Dust. Is this what she was seeing?

Her head felt like it was going to split open. She looked to her side, feeling Rosa's intense gaze bore into her. *Your mind is opening.* Sarah squeezed her eyes shut, as the pain spread over her skull. *Don't fight it, Mija.* Sarah blew out and opened her eyes slowly. The intimidating woman was still looking at her and nodded slightly. Sarah felt relief as the pain started to diminish and Rosa finally looked away.

She started to open her mouth, wanting to ask Rosa about her headache, when a loud growl brought her attention back to the conflict outside.

The man had roared, his jowls shaking violently, as he rushed at Will. Will easily avoided the assault and got behind him. He jumped on the man's back and wrapped his muscled arms around the head and throat.

The man's large nostrils flared while he fought to resist Will's hold. He arched back and reached for Will with thick, large hands. He gripped him by the shoulders and flung him over his head.

Will rolled on the dry dirt and skidded on his back, his face grimaced with pain. The man watched, and waited for Will to charge at him.

Will rose to a crouched position and ran -- aiming low for the abdomen. The attacker bent forward, Will's momentum too great to stop. The man hit a nearby pole, the brittle wood shattering from impact. Will dodged the falling pole and ran to grab for the duffel bag that he'd tossed aside earlier.

Sarah remembered Will slinging the black canvas bag over his shoulder when they left the restaurant earlier. In the chaos of the last few minutes, she'd forgotten about the bag until Will reached for it. He pulled a rope out; it was bright white, thick, with the ends anchored to sharp, silvery-white shards of metal.

Will spun one of the tipped ends next to his side and a sharp whistling pierced the air. He smiled, his soiled face mocking the angry man who growled menacingly.

The rope spun faster, the whistling sound whinnying to too high frequencies until it was silent. The dirt clouds rose around him as the man charged heavily toward his direction.

Will snapped the rope and it wrapped around the thick man's torso. The rope tightened; its coiled strands cutting deep into the man's flesh and tainting the white rope with red. The man bellowed in anger as he fell stiffly onto the hard, dry, dirt of the empty lot.

Will pulled on the other end of the rope. He had control of the man now and he yanked, constricting the cords even tighter around the man.

The wrapped man shrieked and convulsed as his eyes bulged out of their sockets; and the dust thickened, and swirled around the adversaries.

Her view had been completely blocked from sight and she could no longer hear anything outside. Sarah couldn't breathe as she looked on. What was happening? Where was Will? Was he safe?

When the sandstorm finally died down, everything was eerily calm and the heaviness in the air had disappeared, along with Will and the captured man.

Sarah's face was paling. "Oh my god! Will! Where is he?" She could feel the blood draining from her face.

"They're both gone!" Sam's voice was shaking. "What? How?"

Rosa backed away from the window to sit at one of the empty chairs near her. She was fanning herself with her left hand as she continued to make the sign of the cross with her right. When she stopped fanning, she balled her hand into a fist and shook it towards the window. "Vete al infierno, demonio!"

"Ow!" Sarah yelped. Sam was gripping her arm. Her nails piercing flesh. Sam was petrified, looking at the swaying curtain covering the back room behind the counter. Sarah tried to swallow down her fear, but her heart felt like it had jumped into her throat to run for escape. She wrapped Sam in her arms as she tried to slow her breath.

Someone else was inside the restaurant and they had nowhere to run.

The curtain flew up from a gust of air and Will walked out covered in sweat and dirt. The rope he used was now neatly bundled and casually slung over a shoulder, much like the towel he'd used earlier. Sarah looked away as a ray bounced off of the highly polished metal tips of the rope, its brightness almost blinding in its whiteness.

Will set down the rope and Sarah's whole body eased with relief to see him safe and back with them. Why did she care so much? She didn't even know him and he didn't know them, but he protected them from that man.

Sam ran to Will and gave him an excited hug. "You were incredible! Are you ok? What happened to that man? Where did you go? How'd you get back in here?" Her voice was still shaky and Sarah caught her wiping away some tears.

"All these questions will get you in trouble, Señorita," Will replied softly.

"You are totally aggravating. Why don't you ever answer me? If you just told me what was going on, I wouldn't have to ask so many questions," Sam sniffed.

"It's better if you don't know."

"Will, thank you for saving Sam and me... out there." Sarah's heart was beating wildly. She could feel Will's energy surround her, embrace her, even though she could see that he was standing across the room.

"No thanks needed. It's my job." Will smiled and dipped his head. "I'll borrow Rosa's motorcycle and take you both back to the border. We need to hurry. Please, meet me out back."

Will disappeared behind the curtain again and soon after they could hear the rumbling of an engine revving to life.

Sam started to walk toward the counter. "Our ride is ready."

Sarah nodded, kneeling in front of Rosa, taking one of her large hands and holding it between hers. She looked into Rosa's eyes, and with all the sincerity she could pour into her Spanish, she said, "Muchas gracias por todo, Señora! Thank you for everything!" She wished she knew how to say something more meaningful, but her Spanish was basic at best.

She knew that whatever Rosa had done when they returned to the restaurant protected the restaurant from harm. She didn't know how she knew, but she did. There was no doubt in her mind. Without Rosa's help, they would have still been vulnerable to an attack.

For the first time that afternoon, Rosa gave her a smile; a big toothy smile that showed off the gap between her front teeth. "Ten cuidado, Mija. Be careful!" Rosa placed her free hand on top of Sarah's and gave her a gentle squeeze of acknowledgement.

"Sarah, we have to go," Sam interrupted. "Thank you, Rosa."

"Go, go, go now." Rosa waved them on.

The girls headed for the curtain toward the back of the restaurant where Will was waiting. He revved the motorcycle's engine, making black puffs of smoke choke out of the pipe that extended beyond the rear wheel.

Sarah looked at the motorcycle and wondered what Will had in mind. It was a small motorcycle and although it fit him fine by himself...

"How are we supposed to fit on that thing?!" Sam asked.

"Easy. Sarah in front of me, you behind," Will stated matter-of-factly.

"You are totally kidding!" her friend exclaimed.

"No, get on. Hurry. We can't waste time."

The girls looked at each other. Skepticism was written all over their faces, but what choice did they have?

Will extended his arm towards Sarah. She took his hand and let him lead her in front of him. She side straddled the small space in front of Will and he leaned forward to grab the motorcycle's handlebars.

He scooted in further allowing Sam to have a little bit more room behind him. Sam hopped on and straddled the seat behind him. The little motorcycle sank down further, aggravating the small worn out shocks, making them squeal in protest.

Will turned his head slightly towards Sam. "Hang on." The engine revved and the motorcycle awkwardly ambled forward.

Sam grabbed Will around the waist. "Aach! Easy dude! You got precious cargo here," she shouted above the noisy roar of the engine.

Will weaved in and out of traffic within the Avenida and did everything he could to keep from stopping. Sarah slid into Will's open arms as they drove through traffic. She felt safe there, protected, enclosed within a shield of muscles. Her eyes turned up, studying the contour of his chiseled jaw, the high cheekbones, and the ebony hair. She could feel his heart beating next to her, telling her he would be there to watch over her.

They stopped a block away from the border and found a spot to park the motorcycle. He straightened and pulled back from the handlebars to open up and give Sarah room to hop down. She moved slowly, not wanting to lose the physical contact they had during the too short of a motorcycle ride. Sam got off without hesitation; easing the burdened shocks and making the cycle spring up.

"You know what sucks?" Sam sounded completely annoyed as she pursed her lip into a pout. "I never got a picture of a zonkey!"

Sarah couldn't help but laugh. The zonkey was a delightful thought after such a horrid afternoon. She was amazed at Sam's resilience. Wasn't it just a few minutes ago that she sat petrified next to Sarah? And now, she seemed unfazed.

"Zonkey?" Will asked Sarah.

"Don't ask." She smirked as she hooked her friend's arm. The last thing she needed was for Sam to run in search of a zonkey. "Thank you, Will. I wish there was something we could give you or do for you -- for what you did. You were incredible!" She could feel her face warming.

"I'll be in the States after the summer is over. Maybe we can all hang out." Will smiled, his deep dimples making him more irresistible.

Sam quickly pulled out of Sarah's light hold and ran to him.

"Sam!" Sarah gasped out.

Sam pulled a pen out of her backpack and scrawled Sarah's telephone number on his palm. "Call her!" She winked, hurrying back to Sarah.

Will beamed. "You better go. I'll watch from here. I can't cross with you."

The girls slowly walked toward the line of people waiting to cross the border. Sarah looked back, wanting to look at Will for as long as possible. He was leaning against the motorcycle, his gaze diligently scanning the area before locking in on her and giving her a slight bow of his head.

2 CHAPTER TWO
THREE WEEKS LATER,
EARLY AUGUST 1984

Three weeks had felt like a lifetime of painful absence.

He sat on Sam's front stoop, tapping his foot on painted steps that led to the bright red front door of the ornately detailed house. It reminded Will of a dollhouse; tall, steep, and with too much color. He preferred the simple houses of his home town -- bright white stucco that gleamed beneath the rays of the Grecian sun. He missed his home and his mother, but he needed to stay away.

His days with Rosa had been about study and practice. She kept a close, protective watch over him. "Too many dangers Cuervito," she would say to him. Little Crow -- the nickname made sense later, though in the beginning he was perplexed by the choice. Rosa had become his guardian, his mentor, and a trusted friend. If it hadn't been for Rosa's instructions, he would have been lost... and alone... never understanding his purpose.

He still couldn't believe it himself, but after taking a spirit walk under Rosa's guidance he knew what he was meant for. He was of the Carrion Angels and their totem was the raven. Rosa's eyes had grown so big at the revelation, he was afraid they would fall out. "Los Oscuros, the Dark Ones." She had let those words come out in whisper, her breathy tone full of mystery. Then she had slapped his shoulder and smiled wide. "Si. Cuervito."

It all made sense after that. His purpose. His destiny. He'd even seen a glimpse of his future, and what he'd seen was his true mate's radiant energy embracing his very essence and uniting with him in this life.

It had been three weeks since the American girls had come into Rosa's restaurant. That had been a surprise. The restaurant was not visible to all. In fact, only those with unique sight could see and enter into Rosa's domain.

Rosa had been disconcerted. She did not like strangers in her midst, but for him it had been a breath of fresh, revitalizing air. The moment he'd seen Sarah, the past was remembered. He saw familiar energy cascading around her and he knew she was the one from his vision. It was *her*. She was the most beautiful thing he'd ever laid eyes on, a dark haired angel with exotic eyes. When he saw her sitting in Rosa's restaurant, to say that his breath was ripped from his lungs would have been an understatement.

She had a stranger's face, but her spirit and her soul felt intimately close to his. She didn't know who she truly was, but he did.

He'd found the missing piece of himself, but did she feel the same way? God, he prayed that she did. He'd wished their meeting could have been a normal one, but normal was no longer an operative word in his life.

He hadn't been able to stop thinking about her. He had to see her again, even from a distance, but he knew he wouldn't be able to stay away once she was near. She pulled his energy into her, drawing him in with an unseen force that bound him to her. She already owned him.

He blew out and rubbed his palms together. He'd never felt this nervous before. He could feel Samantha's energy inside the house. She was excited, giddy almost. They'd talked earlier and Sam had suggested he wait at her house. He would've waited inside, but he couldn't sit still and he could tell it was making Sam's mother nervous.

Sam poked her head out of the door, jarring him out of his thoughts. "She's on her way," she giggled.

He smiled; he never would have thought that he and Samantha would get this close so quickly. They were exact opposites, but Sam had a way of wearing down the toughest barriers. She was insistent, opinionated, pesky, and had an incredible heart of gold.

Samantha had returned to Tijuana, alone, a few days after he'd seen them off to the border. She'd camped out at the restaurant day and night, until Rosa agreed to talk to her about that fateful day when they'd all met. His mentor could have easily kicked her out, but Samantha's charms had gotten to her, too.

He chuckled, remembering Rosa's bright red mouth dropping to the floor when Sam finally revealed why she was really there. She wanted to learn magick, she wanted to produce real magick and not like the kind you see on stage. "I know what I saw." Sam declared. She stared Rosa down, challenging her to deny the events of that day. She'd seen it, seen the power coming out of Rosa's hands and spreading through the walls of the restaurant. And then there was Will and his fight with the crazy, creepy man that she knew was not "human."

He hadn't been sure how Rosa would respond. Rosa worked alone, and until he came along, she had never taken on any students. The enigmatic Rosa was incredibly powerful -- a sorceress and she possessed the understanding of life forces and its connection to true magick. She practiced an ancient art that her family had preserved but was extinct to everyone else.

He'd been the first to be given the privilege and honor of becoming her student, but as Rosa had confided in him, she was the last of her line and didn't want the art to die with her. She had to make sure it was passed on to someone worthy. He didn't think that Rosa had foreseen she would be teaching more than one.

The unyielding woman had finally met her Achilles heel in a bubbly package named Samantha Montclair. He remembered Rosa groaning, when she finally conceded to teach the young woman, but she had to test Samantha first -- to determine her strengths.

Rosa explained that everyone had the capability to craft magick, but some were stronger than others and came into it more naturally and with more power.

He had no doubt Sam would be powerful one day. He'd seen her energy, too. Sam carried traces of ancient magick within her; traces of forgotten abilities that had lain dormant for generations. It was no surprise to him that she'd found them again. Sam was remembering, waking up to her lost lineage of magick.

She worked hard while she'd stayed with them and gained his respect quickly. Sam was a quick study in many things, but had to work really hard to conjure magick itself.

"She has a noisy mind. She needs to quiet herself in several ways and she will be incredible," the sorceress had said with a chuckle. "You better watch it Cuervito, she will get you back for always trying to spark her hair on fire."

He'd had fun teasing Sam and throwing energy sparks at her. He chuckled, thinking of Sam's infuriated look when he'd aim a spark right at her hair.

She would waggle her finger at him. "Unless you can put out fire with your mojo, I would suggest you not aim for my coif," she'd warn with a laugh. "It's flammable."

He'd shrug and change his aim and go for her bare feet, making her hop around. He'd burst out laughing to see her dance around, trying to avoid his sparks. "This is for your training!"

"You're not funny." She would stick out her tongue and throw little sparks at him that would fizzle out as soon as it hit the air. "Aaargh! You are so aggravating."

Though he'd been a little disappointed that she'd come alone, Sam had talked about Sarah so much it had felt as if she was there. The more he heard about Sam's best friend, the more he began to believe she really was the one.

When Sam left to return to San Francisco almost a week ago, the restaurant grew quiet and Rosa admittedly missed Sam's presence. So did he.

He missed their talks about Sarah.

Sam had called, just this morning, "I've been flaking on her since I got back. She just called. You need to get over here." Sam had urged him to *jump* to San Francisco to see Sarah. "If I know my best friend, she'll be coming over here to check on me and then chew me out!"

He begged Rosa to let him go to San Francisco. She never really kept him from doing anything, but doing something with her approval was much better than going against her will. He'd made the *jump* easily. All he had to do was think of Sarah, and he was pulled to the city.

Now, he was right where he needed to be.

His hands were clammy and his guts were twisting with anxiety. He was getting impatient. He needed to move and decided to walk up the hill, toward Sarah's house. He'd almost made it to the top of the hill when he saw her hair, glistening in the sun. His heart stopped and jumped to his throat, tightening his vocal cords, making him clear his throat to free his airway.

She was breathtaking, as radiant as the energy surrounding her. He wanted to reach out to touch her face, to feel the softness of her cheek against his rough hands. He couldn't think. It was hard to speak and all he wanted to do was bask in her energy.

"Is it really you?" She smiled, her voice sounding as if butterflies were tickling her insides. Sarah grabbed his forearm and squeezed, checking to make sure he was real.

Will smiled, feeling his dimples deepen. "I caught you at a bad time?"

"I was on my way to Sam's. Do you want to come with me?" Sam had been right about predicting Sarah's reaction.

"Umm. Yes, I would love that, but I shouldn't." He had promised Sam that he would keep Sarah away from her house. *If she gets to my house, then I can't lie to her! Sam had pleaded with him. She gives me that look and I just can't do it! I'll tell her about all my hocus-pocus activities… I swear, but I need to find the right time to do it. I don't want to freak her out.* He understood Sam's predicament. It was never easy, to reveal true magick to anyone. "I'm not supposed to be here, but I had to see you."

There were too many questions in Sarah's eyes. "You're not supposed to be here? What do you mean?"

"I wanted to… I needed to see you again."

"Did you jump the border? Are you going to be deported?!"

Will grinned at her panic, assuring her that was not the issue. "Can we go somewhere to talk? If you can't, I understand." It was a miracle he could respond to her at all. Was that his voice talking? It sounded too soft, apologetic, unsure.

33

"If I go, can I ask you some questions about that day?" Sarah was looking for information, just as much as Sam had been.

Was her heart pounding so hard she could feel her rib cage vibrate? His was. "Yes, of course."

Sarah led him to a nearby café where they could sit and talk in peace. The large glass window of the shop was warmly lit with golden lights that sparkled against the glass. They walked in and he instantly felt the tickle of a barrier rubbing against his energy. The café had shields around it. He pushed out his own barriers, testing the shields around him. The shields were strong.

Someone here was from magick.

He noticed the totems spread around the small coffee shop. They were made to look like kitschy decoration, but he knew better. The totems were sources of power, thrumming with energy. He instinctively went into a defensive mode.

Sarah looked at him, her eyes bright as her smile. "This is where I like to study. Something about the ambiance in this place really gets my creative juices flowing."

Will followed her to an empty table and pulled out a chair next to the aisle for her. He took the seat across from her, with his back against a wall and where he could clearly see the entirety of the small café. He scanned the room, reading each of the patrons that sat around them.

"Do a lot of people come here?" he asked.

"Umm, mostly just regulars. I always see the same people."

"Do you know the owner?"

"A little. She's really nice. That's her over there." Sarah pointed to a petite woman with long flowing blond hair and deep brown eyes.

She looked delicate and otherworldly.

The café owner twisted her willowy frame towards their table. She was staring at Will, her eyes brightening. *You are safe here.* A soothing, melodic voice echoed in his mind as the beautiful woman bowed to them before turning away to speak with another patron.

Sarah's brows twisted, confusion shadowing her eyes as she looked at Will. "Did you hear that?" She was looking around, trying to find the source of the mysterious voice.

He didn't answer. Now that the café owner had accepted him as a friend, he could focus on Sarah. He wanted to just watch her and sear her beauty into his memory to always have her near.

She was nervous, but so was he. More than he'd ever been in his twenty years.

She turned to him, "Do you know her, the owner?"

Will shook his head. "I've never met her before, but I can see why you like it here. It's very cozy."

She cleared her throat, "Sooo, what are you doing in San Francisco?"

"I wanted to see you again." Will's voice was a hushed whisper. How do you tell someone you've just met that you've been in love with them? How do you tell a stranger that you've been together before -- in past lives?

Rosa had told him that each lifetime was unique. That even if they'd been mates before, didn't mean they would be again in this life. He hadn't wanted to hear it. What would he do if she was meant for another in this life? Could he live knowing the missing part of his soul was with another?

He reached for her hands and held them lightly, his thumbs stroking her fingers. "What did you want to ask me?"

She straightened in her seat, "What happened in Tijuana?" She didn't hesitate with her question.

He looked at their entwined hands for a long time. "You witnessed something that should have been hidden from you, but… you were able to see."

"Hidden? Your fight was out in the open. Rosa… in the restaurant… " Her mind seemed to be turning over a thousand questions.

"I don't know that I'm the right person to provide you with an explanation." He was still learning and he hoped he could find the right words, "There's a world steeped with power and wonder, and you're a part of it. I'm just beginning to understand my part in it." He turned his head away for a moment and then locked his gaze back onto Sarah.

"What are you saying, Will?" she looked confused.

"You are a rare diamond, extremely unique… special." It was time. "Close your eyes. Trust me." He connected with her subconscious and opened up his mind to show her what he had seen -- the glimpse of their union. Would she know that radiant energy was her own? He prayed she would.

Her fingers tightened around his. Her essence opened with his touch. He felt her powers surge into him like a storm, gripping every fiber of his being, making his heart clench as their energies merged and they lived their lifetimes together in one breath.

She opened her eyes slowly as he felt the walls that she kept tightly gartered around her fall away. He knew that her heart had instantly recognized that the man sitting across from her was her other half. She was remembering that she'd always been his. He sensed the swelling of her heart while all her feelings for him rose from within her soul, waking up forgotten memories of past lives spent with the man before her.

He brought her hands to his lips and kissed the tops of her hands slowly. "My beautiful angel," he whispered into his kiss.

I love you. It was a whisper sent by her heart. There was no reason or logic to this moment; that she would love a stranger with her entire being, or that he would love her the same… but it was true, and that was all that mattered. *I'm yours and I will love you eternally,* she whispered in his mind. Her voice was a soothing balm on his soul, anointing every part of his being, reminding him that he was now whole and he was loved.

We are one Sarah. I knew you the moment I saw you. Their minds and their hearts were one, once again. Their union was inevitable, as sure as the stars burned in the sky. He felt like crying. He was overcome with joy. She'd accepted him and they would be together.

He held her gaze and kissed her hand again, her perfumed lotion filling his senses, like her energy had filled his soul.

Her energy was closing, slowly shrinking back, and separating to bring her completely back into her own.

He felt the weight of another vision bearing down on him. He dipped his head and closed his eyes, gripped by the images rushing into his mind. He clasped her hand tightly while his heart thundered, making him sweat.

This vision was his to bear and he kept it from her, even as she opened her essence up to him, comforting him, and letting him feel her eternal love for him.

"Will, is everything okay?" her voice was trembling.

He nodded quickly, as a crystalline voice began to fade into the recesses of his mind. *Protect them, protect them at all cost.*

He'd been given another glimpse of his future. A child would be born in this lifetime, a special one; the only one that he and Sarah would ever have. This child would be born under a raging storm, a great power that will bear the might of all four elements… He tried to hold on to the vision, to *see* more of what may come, but it ended too quickly.

He wasn't given enough information to know what might lay ahead for him and his future family. *Protect them, protect them at all cost.* His heart twinged at the resonant voice in his mind and he pledged his soul to uphold the command.

He looked up, finally released from the intensity of the vision. Sarah had moved and was sitting next to him. She looked him over, concern dimming her bright energy. "I'm okay." He reassured her.

She let her breath go and pulled him into an embrace as tears streamed down her cheeks. "You scared me. I thought I was going to lose you already."

He leaned his forehead on hers and closed his eyes, letting her energy soothe him. He caught her faltering breath in a tender kiss.

"I love you," she sighed against his lips.

The prelude to their life had begun.

~~ ## ~~

(left blank on purpose)

ABOUT THE AUTHOR

Cecily Magnon is from the fertile valleys of northern California, where she lives with her husband and kids, and gets inspired by the diversity, beauty, and bounty of the people and of the land around her.

A self-proclaimed nerd girl, Cecily has had a fascination with all topics outside of the norm since she was a little girl. Things of fantasy, magick, sci-fi, the supernatural, and day dreams are the juice that nourishes her imagination and infuse into her writing.

According to Cecily, there is no such thing as "ordinary" when you *believe* and you *see* that the everyday is filled with magick.

BOOKS FROM CECILY MAGNON

I am not Frazzle
(Cecily is a contributing author to this collection of short stories. All proceeds go to the Devizes Children's Centre.)

Prelude to a Storm
(Prequel to Gathering Storm)

Gathering Storm: Order of the Anakim

Dark Skies: Order of the Anakim
(Coming soon!)

(left blank on purpose)

Made in the USA
San Bernardino, CA
13 September 2014